Diego Saves Christmas!

adapted by Alexis Romay

based on the original teleplay by Chris Gifford

illustrated by Art Mawhinney

Simon Spotlight/Nick Jr.

New York   London   Toronto   Sydney

Based on the TV series *Go, Diego, Go!*™ as seen on Nick Jr.®

SIMON SPOTLIGHT
An imprint of Simon & Schuster Children's Publishing Division
1230 Avenue of the Americas, New York, New York 10020
© 2007 Viacom International Inc. All rights reserved.
NICK JR., *Go, Diego, Go!*, and all related titles, logos, and characters are registered
trademarks of Viacom International Inc.
All rights reserved, including the right of reproduction in whole or in part in any form.
SIMON SPOTLIGHT and colophon are registered trademarks of Simon & Schuster, Inc.
Nontoxic
Manufactured in the United States of America
First Edition
2 4 6 8 10 9 7 5 3 1
ISBN-13: 978-1-4169-4210-8
ISBN-10: 1-4169-4210-6

¡Hola! I'm Diego. *¡Feliz Navidad!* Merry Christmas! It's Christmas Eve at the Animal Rescue Center! Everyone is waiting for Santa to bring presents. I'm hoping for a new telescope!

We work extra hard here for Christmas because many animals are away from their natural homes and families. Sometimes the animals worry that Santa won't find them. That's why we put these Santa signs in front of their homes.

That sounds like animals in trouble. They need our help! Come on!

We need our special camera, Click, to find the animals who need our help.

Say "Click!" Click has two pictures of animals. The animals that need our help make this sound: "Heowww! Heowww!" Do you see an animal that makes this sound?

The reindeer are trying to pull a sleigh with presents, but it's stuck in that snow on the mountain. If Santa can't get his sleigh out of that snow, he won't be able to deliver his Christmas presents!

We need to find a strong animal to help us climb up the mountain and pull the sleigh out of the snow.

Which of these animals is strong, great at climbing, and can pull heavy things?

¡Sí! The llama can pull Santa's sleigh out of the snow!

Llamas live on mountains and eat grass, so that's where we should look for a llama. Do you see any grass on the mountain? Yeah! There's my friend Linda the Llama.

¡Al rescate! To the rescue!
Let's save Christmas!

I can't see with all this dust! But Linda can! Llamas can see through the dust because they have long eyelashes that block out the dirt. We need to use field goggles to block out the dirt so we can find Linda! Make field goggles with your hands! *¡Excelente!*

Look! I see the llamas taking a dust bath! They want to be clean for when Santa gets here! Let's call to Linda! Say, *"¡Hola, Linda!"*

Linda will help us get Santa's sleigh out of the snow! *¡Fantástico!*

Let's climb up the mountain with Linda!

¡Cuidado! Careful! The ice is very slippery. But Linda can walk without slipping on the ice. Look at her feet!

Llamas have padded feet that keep them from slipping on the ice!

We made it to Santa and his reindeer! Now we need Linda to help pull the stuck sleigh out of the snow so that Santa can deliver the Christmas presents. Say, "*¡Hala, Linda!* Pull, Linda!"

To thank Linda for getting his sleigh out, Santa sprinkled magic
Christmas sparkles over her so she can fly!

Now we can deliver the presents to all of our friends and family!

¡Misión cumplida! Rescue complete! We couldn't have saved Christmas without your help! *¡Feliz Navidad!* Merry Christmas!